Subject to Fits

(a response to Dostoyevsky's *The Idiot*)

by Robert Montgomery

SAMUELFRENCH.COM

No one shall commit or authorize any act or omission by which the copyright of, or the right to copyright, this play may be impaired.
No one shall make any changes in this play - words or music - for the purpose of production.
Publication of this play does not imply availability for performance. Both amateurs and professionals considering a production are strongly advised in their own interests to apply to Samuel French, Inc., for written permission before starting rehearsals, advertising, or booking a theatre.
No part of this book may be reproduced, stored in a retrieval system, or transmitted in any form, by any means, now known or yet to be invented, including mechanical, electronic, photocopying, recording, videotaping, or otherwise, without the prior written permission of the publisher.

MUSIC MATERIALS

The orchestration consisting of **Organ/Conductor Score, Cello, Bass, and Vocal Score** is available from Samuel French, Inc.

Please contact Samuel French for more information, perusal of the music materials, and a performance license application.

IMPORTANT BILLING AND CREDIT REQUIREMENTS

All producers of *SUBJECT TO FITS must* give credit to the Author/ Composer of the Play in all programs distributed in connection with performances of the Play, and in all instances in which the title of the Play appears for the purposes of advertising, publicizing or otherwise exploiting the Play and/or a production. The name of the Author *must* appear on a separate line on which no other name appears, immediately following the title and *must* appear in size of type not less than fifty percent of the size of the title type.

CHARACTERS

MYSHKIN - a child-like epileptic

ROGOZHIN - a wealthy dissipate

LEBEDEV - a money-grubbing toady

NATASHA - a wild high-society woman

MME. YEPANCHIN - maternal, good-hearted

AGLAYA YEPANCHIN - her daughter, pretty and volatile

GANYA IVOGLIN - a mediocre social climber

IPPOLIT IVOGLIN - an extremely sensitive consumptive

GENERAL IVOGLIN - a very alcoholic storyteller

AUTHOR'S NOTE

Subject to Fits is neither adaptation, dramatization nor translation of Dostoyevsky's inimitable novel *The Idiot.* The greatness of Dostoyevsky's masterpiece is inseparable from its novelistic form, and any attempt to transpose it literally into another art form could not help but undermine its wholeness and alienate its power. *Subject to Fits* is a response to *The Idiot:* it is absolutely unfaithful to the novel; it uses the novel for its own selfish purposes; it does not hold the novel responsible. As such, it is its own work – smacking of *The Idiot,* dreaming of *The Idiot,* but mostly, taking off from where *The Idiot* drove it.

*This work is gratefully dedicated first to Dr. Thomas Haas
and finally to A.J. Antoon.*

ACT I

Overture: **EAGLES SCREAM**, *which turns into a fly.
The music comes from an organ, a cello, and an electric
bass.*

Lights up on **PRINCE MYSHKIN**, *in a [glass] box,
simple, but worried. And* **MME. YEPANCHIN**, *direct but
worried.*

MME. YEPANCHIN. Dear Prince. We have this neurosis of
trying to understand everything about everybody. We
come to St. Peterburg, our experiential slate clean as a
baby's. In one mad day we are injected with the demo-
cratic idea of Natasha Fillipovna; we fall in love with
Aglaya; we meet a group of insane characters straight
out of the contemporary Russian novel, all of whom
bombard us with ideas and experiences which are in
no way connected to one another. Add to this epilepsy, and the large sunspots that appeared that day
for the first time since the Aquarian comet and you
gather all this in indiscriminately, and decide to base
the rest of your life rearranging that one day into perfect harmony! You see how it fits, Prince? You see how
everything fits?!

MYSHKIN. Heehaw! *(He laughs.)*

(Blackout: Music: **FITTING**, *turning into a train.*
MYSHKIN *is laughing.* **ROGOZHIN** *and* **LEBEDEV** *are
seated next to him.* **ROGOZHIN** *barks at* **MYSHKIN**.
They look at each other. They laugh together.)

ROGOZHIN. Excuse me – for some reason I've taken a
strong liking to you. Forgive me – I'm somewhat delirious from a fever. I keep hearing dogs in my head.

MYSHKIN. I forgive you for liking me, and assure you, the kinship I feel with you already is deeper than the blood in your eyes, and stronger than the murder on your face. Prince Lyov Myshkin, your servant, sir.

LEBEDEV. A prince! Have you a ring to kiss, Prince?

MYSHKIN. I'm sorry, I have neither money, parents, nor baggage. I am a simple person whose only purpose is to go to St. Petersburg and get to know as many human beings as possible. I've just undergone treatment in the desert for epilepsy and –

LEBEDEV. Ohhhh! Prince Twitch! Perhaps you've shaken some brains out through your ears, eh, "Prince?" Why, your title alone must be worth its weight in farts! Haw-haw –

MYSHKIN. *(laughing with him)* You're really remarkable – but I suppose you know far better than I how extraordinarily repulsive you are – here, there's something coming out of your nose… *(reaches for it)*

LEBEDEV. Get away from me, you idiot!!

(Train whistle. ROGOZHIN *shoves* LEBEDEV.*)*

ROGOZHIN. Call me Rogozhin, Prince.

LEBEDEV. Paryfon Rogozhin? Pray let Lebedev grovel at your wealthy feet!

ROGOZHIN. *(kicking him away)* You can dance on your head in manure if you want!

LEBEDEV. *(dancing)* I will! Don't give me a kopeck! I'm leaving my wife and five children just to dance on manure for you!

MYSHKIN. He's sincere!

ROGOZHIN. Hang him! When sincerity comes to that, I'll kill my best friend.

MYSHKIN. And love your enemy?

ROGOZHIN. *(shivering spastically)* Godammit, I'd better not be dying!

(Train whistle. Blackout. In the darkness, we hear AGLAYA *giggling and:)*

MME. YEPANCHIN. You're the one who has fits, aren't you?

(Lights up. **MYSHKIN** *visiting the Yepanchin household.)*

And you claim to be the last of the Prince Myshkins since my brother died? ...And you have fits.

AGLAYA. Maman, have him tell us a story!

MYSHKIN. Your face, Madame Yepanchin, tells me you are a perfect child.

MME. YEPANCHIN. See how well he pronounces his words! You fascinate me, Prince – are you quiet about it or do your arms shake around?

AGLAYA. Tell us a story about the desert, Prince, or leave this house immediately.

MYSHKIN. I had just recovered from epilepsy and everything seemed alien and hostile. I was afraid I'd be arrested if I stood on any one patch of sand too long. The fact that the sun was warm... worried me. And every time night came, I felt it was my fault. Then one morning I heard the braying of a donkey in the marketplace, and suddenly everything was familiar. I was sure I had seen the world before, and with a great happiness, I realized I wasn't responsible for anything.

AGLAYA. *(giggling highly)* A donkey! A donkey!

MME. YEPANCHIN. Aglaya! Now what is so absurd? Many women fell in love with animals in mythology.

*(**MYSHKIN** begins laughing with **AGLAYA**.)*

MYSHKIN. It's nice the way I laugh sometimes, don't you think? *(to **MME. YEPANCHIN**)* And you want me to know you're very fond of Aglaya even though she's frivolous and just like you!

*(**AGLAYA** stops laughing; **MYSHKIN** & **MME. YEPANCHIN** laugh now.)*

I understand you totally!

MME. YEPANCHIN. *(through her laughter)* I am a good person! You and I, Prince – we're the exact same child! Poor Aglaya. *(kisses **AGLAYA**)*

AGLAYA. Prince, teach us how to be happy.

MYSHKIN. *(looking at her really for the first time, falling in love)* Pretty.

AGLAYA. Do you think you live better than anyone else?

MYSHKIN. Yes.

AGLAYA. Anyone like you should be happy forever! You'll lie in your grave thinking how lovely it is to have such nice bones for neighbors! Show you an execution or a deck of cards and you'll draw sublime conclusions from both.

MYSHKIN. I have seen an execution. The guillotine. The blade – the man heard it scraping down toward his neck. I saw him. As his head was falling off, it suddenly realized – it was falling off. I couldn't tell – no matter how hard I tried – I couldn't tell what the chopped head was thinking in the six seconds it remained alive, before it stopped its careful rocking and grew still.

*(**MME. YEPANCHIN** squeals; **AGLAYA** smiles.)*

AGLAYA. You haven't told me what you think about my face, Prince.

*(Blackout. Knocking. **GANYA** enters with lit candle.)*

MYSHKIN. Are you Ganya, Madame Yepanchin's manservant?

GANYA. Yes I am, you drooling mongoloid – what do you want?

MYSHKIN. Aglaya told me you had a room to let.

GANYA. You talked to Aglaya? She's some treasure, eh? *(pulls out a picture of **NATASHA FILLIPOVNA**)* But she's worth nothing compared to this one – look at her! Why, her breasts alone are worth several factories!

MYSHKIN. She's seen an execution.

GANYA. A real piece of eight, if you know what I mean.

MYSHKIN. I am not a man of the world, sir.

GANYA. You're an idiot, that's what you are – gravy-brains!

MYSHKIN. Sir, you are more unlike a child than any man I have ever met. I am no more deranged than you are happy. I learn nothing new about myself from your insults. *(turns to leave)*

GANYA. Don't go! You alone must know how I detest my mediocrity! Here is your room. Please, accept these kopecks as a token of my character. My drunken father will be up presently, and my disgusting little brother who is consumptive.

(**GANYA** *exits. Enter* **IVOGLIN** *and* **IPPOLIT**.)

IVOGLIN. What is this sight that turns these petrified eyes of mine into pudding? Could it be – yes! – Prince … Vitchnickskivitchstoy MUSHKIN!! It's General Ivoglin! *(They embrace.)* I used to hold you in my arms when you were but a wee worm of a babe! Your father and I used to save each other's lives in the wars. I would have killed him in a duel for the fair hand of your mother, but we both missed intentionally and ended up in each other's arms, leaving your mother crying by herself in the wind as we frolicked off to the nearest vodka house!

IPPOLIT. Two months to live. Two cramped months of thin pink blood and golden fat servings of phlegm!

IVOGLIN. This is Ippolit, my son! I used to hold him in my arms when he was but a wee worm of a babe.

IPPOLIT. Should I learn a trade? Carpentry, of course! I should have time to build a toothpick! I vow, Prince, if I don't figure out, before I die, why I should be living – I shall commit suicide!

MYSHKIN. In China I was told the story of a man who contracted tuberculosis at the age of fifteen, and was told he had but eight months to live. He quit school, deserted all his friends, and began soul-searching for a reason to continue living. When the eight months were up, he was told he had but four days left to live. He spent the four days contemplating suicide. On the fourth day, he was told he had but eight months to

live. When he was forty years old, he was told he had
but four weeks to live. When he was sixty years old, he
was told he had but ten years to live. Still he refused
to learn or converse, so intent was he on his purpose
of life. At the age of seventy (after being told he had
but eight months to live), he suddenly felt as if a huge
blade were hanging over his head. At seventy-two, he
put a pistol to his head, held it there, thought for a
while, held it there for eight hours, had a heart attack,
and died. He wasn't even aware of the change.

IVOGLIN. Marvelous! Bravo! Your father and I used to tell
that story to each other for hours on end! Never tire
of it! Ah, Prince – Prince?! One day you shall be King!
(*Extends his palm;* **IPPOLIT** *is coughing.*)

MYSHKIN. Please, General – take these kopecks and buy
some spiced wine – for Ippolit's coughing and your
own nerves.

IVOGLIN. My blessings, son – already I love you more that I
loved Napoleon!

(**IVOGLIN** *and* **IPPOLIT** *exit.*

Knocking. Music: **NATASHA FILLIPOVNA**. *More
insistent knocking by* **NATASHA**. **MYSHKIN** *opens the
door. He is crushed by* **NATASHA**'s *beauty. They stare at
each other.* **NATASHA** *flings her coat at him.*)

NATASHA. Do you realize how long I've been waiting?
Some servants should be tortured! With knives!
(**MYSHKIN** *drops her coat.*) Now he's dropped my coat!
Good God, fool – if I had your hands I'd eat with my
feet! (**MYSHKIN** *picks up the coat.*) Well? Go along and
announce me. Why are you carrying my coat like that?

(**MYSHKIN** *drags her coat back.* **NATASHA** *laughs.*
MYSHKIN *does, too. He drops the coat again.*)

Ha-hah, he's dropped it again! You aren't an epileptic
idiot by any chance, are you?

(**MYSHKIN** *again laughs with her, nodding. She stamps
her foot.*)

What are you laughing at? Announce me!

(**MYSHKIN** *goes off.*)

Wait, idiot! How can you announce me if you don't know my name?

MYSHKIN. Natasha Fillipovna!

(*They stare.* **NATASHA** *freezes gracefully.* **MYSHKIN** *strides into the* **IVOGLIN***s, announces:*)

NATASHA FILLIPOVNA!

(*Re-enter train scene:*)

ROGOZHIN. Natasha Fillipovna is her name!

(*Re-enter Yepanchin scene:*)

AGLAYA. You haven't told me what you thought of my face, Prince.

ROGOZHIN. She is as beautiful as this knife – I would kill anyone who thought of her the same way I do!

(**MYSHKIN** *is bouncing and being bounced in and out of all these scenes.*)

MYSHKIN. (*looking at* **AGLAYA**'*s face*) Aglaya's face is super-latively pretty – she is almost as beautiful as Natasha Fillipovna.

(*Re-enter* **GANYA** *scene:*)

GANYA. (*showing* **MYSHKIN** *a portrait of* **NATASHA***:*) This is a woman named –

MYSHKIN & YEPANCHINS. Natasha Fillipovna!??

GANYA. (*to* **MYSHKIN***)* How do you know her name?

MYSHKIN. (*to* **MME. YEPANCHIN***)* Ganya showed me her por-trait.

AGLAYA. Our gardener's been having an affair with that woman!

LEBEDEV. (*to* **ROGOZHIN & MYSHKIN***)* In the last three months, she's been seen dancing with fourteen noble-men, twelve ambassadors, six blond peasant youths and two blacksmiths!

MYSHKIN. *(to* **GANYA***)* A man on the train described her to me.

ROGOZHIN. I met her at the opera. Or was it a dance hall? No matter, my father found out and died. When she first spoke to me, her breath *came* all over my face.

MYSHKIN. *(to* **GANYA***)* So I recognized her immediately.

ROGOZHIN. Since then, every room I'm in seems filled with steam.

NATASHA. How can you announce me if you don't know my name?!

(*MUSIC:* **NATASHA FILLIPOVNA***.*

Re-re-enter the **IVOGLINS***.*

The director should determine entrances and exits here, depending on the amount of clutter or non-clutter s/he wants, can afford or can stand. The pace of the lines should be murderous, however.)

IVOGLIN. General Mushkin – do you know anything of this Natasha Fillipopnop? Ganya has forbidden us to utter her name in this house.

MYSHKIN. *(to* **GANYA***)* I told Aglaya she was almost as beautiful as Natasha Fillipovna, so her mother wants to see that portrait.

GANYA. Did you tell them my doodle was poking about Natasha Fillipovna's soft plump purse – did you tell them that?

(**MYSHKIN** *has given the portrait to* **MME. YEPANCHIN***;* **AGLAYA** *looks, too.)*

MME. YEPANCHIN. She is somewhat fetching, Prince, but I've seen prettier things on heretical crucifixes.

GANYA. *(to his family and* **MYSHKIN***)* She promised to declare at her birthday party tonight whether she will marry me or no. That's all – we won't speak of it any further.

NATASHA. Announce me!

AGLAYA. "Almost as beautiful," indeed! China crockery!

MME. YEPANCHIN. Prince, call Ganya in – either there's a bad smell of marriage in the air, or the cook burnt the cabbage again.

MYSHKIN. *(to* **GANYA**, *pointing)* Something about Natasha Fillipovna....

IPPOLIT. *(to* **GANYA**) I refuse to fritter away my dying days receiving into my family any woman with the bilious capacity to stomach such an impacted bowel as you!

MME. YEPANCHIN. *(to* **GANYA**, *who's been "called in")* Whom do you plan to marry, young man? It couldn't be Aglaya – *(to* **AGLAYA**) you couldn't possibly cram a honeymoon in this week, could you, child?

GANYA. Who? M-me? M-marry? Whom?

*(***MME. YEPANCHIN*** shoves the portrait in his face.)*

Ohhh! ha-ha! Why here's the picture I found in the gutter outside the Bolstoy House! Ha-ha! I assure you, madame, I earn a surprisingly generous salary, thank you – and, er, consistently laugh at the same jokes as the highest paid officials. I must impress on you, madame, that I'm much too much a respectable, up-and-coming young man to afford marrying a woman so bankrupt in character as this Natasha uh Natasha... Fillerpurseup.

(turns angrily to **IPPOLIT**, *in another scene:)*

Wouldn't you like a coffin when you die? Wouldn't you like a priest to sprinkle some nice pretty hard-working prayers over your sweet-smelling corpse? So how the hell you think we're going to afford your funeral unless I marry Natasha Fillipovna and her thirty-five thousand rubles? You ought to be thankful you're still alive yet ... I thought I heard you die last night in the hallway. *(Imitates coughing. Then, to* **MYSHKIN**, *privately:)* What about this Rogozhin?

*(***ROGOZHIN***, during the above, has appeared and begun drawing his knife flirtatiously across* **NATASHA**'s *throat.)*

MYSHKIN. He has recently become very feverish and quite wealthy. He would marry Natasha Fillipovna tomorrow and cut her throat next week.

NATASHA. *(with **ROGOZHIN***'s *knife at her throat)* Announce me, idiot!

IVOGLIN. *(to **GANYA***) I demand you tell your father who this Fillerupnip is that she considers her unrefined milk the proper food for my grandson!

LEBEDEV. *(exiting train scene)* St. Petersburg! All out for St. Petersburg and the hot breath of –

MYSHKIN. *(announcing)* Natasha Fillipovna!

ROGOZHIN. *(still at **NATASHA***) How about it, Prince? Should I see if Natasha has a friend for you?

MYSHKIN. Oh no – no thank you – on account of my illness, I have never known woman.

(**ROGOZHIN** *laughs and exits.*)

MME. YEPANCHIN. Goodbye, dear Prince – you and I, we're the exact same child. God sent you to St. Petersburg just for me. It's the nicest thing he's ever done. *(exits with **AGLAYA***)

IVOGLIN. *(screaming at **GANYA**, who is protesting loudly, "No –" "Don't you –" etc.)* By right of the fourth commandment, I hereby speak the unspeakable name: Natasha Fillernippup!

(**IPPOLIT** *and* **IVOGLIN** *taunt the name at* **GANYA**, *who is furious.* **MYSHKIN** *comes to them and announces at last for real:)*

MYSHKIN. NATASHA FILLIPOVNA!

GANYA. Who?

(**NATASHA** *enters the Ivoglin household. Stunned silence.*)

NATASHA. Hello, my fond little Ganya. Did you get my portrait? Isn't it dreadful? I had a cold that day. *(gives **IPPOLIT** and **IVOGLIN** a once-over)* So this is the family you'd rather not discuss. *(gives **MYSHKIN** a tip, which he ignores)* You may go now.

MYSHKIN. *(to the agog* GANYA*)* Let me get you a glass of water.

GANYA. *(snapping to)* …What? Ha! And now you're a doctor, eh Prince? Why is everyone acting so confused? *(to* NATASHA*)* This is our lodger, Prince Myshkin – he won't hurt you. Prince Myshkin, this is…uh – ha-ha … of course, it's… *(can't remember – jamais vu)* uh –

MYSHKIN. *(whispering)* Natasha Fillipovna …

GANYA. I KNOW, YOU FOOL! *(to* NATASHA*)* Excuse me, he's a bit – a bit – uhhh –

NATASHA. A prince?

(They look at each other.)

MYSHKIN. I've seen an execution. I couldn't shut my eyes.

NATASHA. Are you aware now that your eyes are open?

MYSHKIN. I have the strangest feeling I've never met you anywhere before in my entire life.

NATASHA. *(after a slight pause)* My uncles never tickled me in the wrong places. My younger sisters often left long letters for me under my pillow. Sometimes my older brothers were rude to me. My mother and father told jokes to each other in the middle of their arguments. If I asked them about gladiators, they gave me picture books about Rome. When I grabbed for pineapple, they gave me lettuce. When I first menstruated, my mother and I were grinning the whole day. Whenever I laughed for no reason at all, my father would not make me explain. I have loved pineapple ever since.

MYSHKIN. You mustn't blame your family. They only did what they thought best for you. Happiness makes you yawn. *(She yawns.)* Do you like me?

NATASHA. *(laughing, breaking away)* And do we want to play bouncy-ball, little poopoo face? Do you want to show me what yours looks like and I'll show you mine? Do we want to read each other's minds for the rest of our lives while all around us babies are being born without legs and beautiful old people are falling in love? I'm not half as interesting as everything else, Prince.

IVOGLIN. If I may say so myself, just last Sunday a vicious hyena escaped from the zoo. Rising to the occasion, I ripped the full-length dress off a nearby lady, made a sack of it, and so captured the inhuman creature.

NATASHA. *(taking his arm)* That's very interesting.

IVOGLIN. Ganya, my son, gives me great pleasure. I have known him since he was a schoolboy.

NATASHA. But more interesting is the story in last Sunday's *Daily Independence* about an anonymous capture of an escaped hyena. And more interesting still is the man found recently who admits to the vulgar heroic.

IVOGLIN. Well … let the poor imposter have his accolades.

NATASHA. And the most interesting thing of all is his eye, which the hyena had clawed out; and his head, which is now up to its ears in pus! *(starts laughing;* IVOGLIN *retreats)*

IPPOLIT. Prince! … *(sputters)* Hit her!

(GANYA *tries to shove* IPPOLIT *out.*

*MUSIC: **ROGOZHIN THEME**. Dramatic entrance:* ROGOZHIN.)

ROGOZHIN. You weren't expecting Paryfon Rogozhin, perhaps!

(Dramatic entrance: LEBEDEV.*)*

LEBEDEV. You weren't expecting Paryfon Rogozhin and Lebedev, perhaps!

(Dramatic announcement: NATASHA*)*

NATASHA. You weren't expecting Natasha Fillipovna, perhaps!

ROGOZHIN. Prince! I wasn't expecting you!

GANYA. Isn't this my house?

ROGOZHIN. *(pulling a knife on* GANYA, *who retreats to* NATASHA*)* Are you marrying him?

NATASHA. I shall announce everything at my birthday party tonight! Perhaps I might even marry the Prince!

IVOGLIN. Of course: Nostalgia Fillerpopnip! I believe I knew your aunt! Long ago we used to picnic and watch you cavort on the grass, innocently naked…. Ahh, how times change ….

GANYA. *(seeing* NATASHA*'s rising irritation)* Father!! *(to* NATASHA*:)* You must excuse him, he's a bit, a bit –

(IPPOLIT *begins coughing violently.)*

Good God, Ippolit! Can't you do that somewhere else –

IPPOLIT. I shall step off this floor only when she scrubs it!! *(coughs in* NATASHA*'s face)*

NATASHA. *(examining what she's wiped off her face)* A fine family, Ganya – and I came here to invite them to my party.

GANYA. *(to* IPPOLIT*)* You're ruining me!! *(goes to slap* IPPOLIT*, is stopped by* MYSHKIN*)* You again! *(slaps* MYSHKIN*: there is a delay before we hear the slap sound and see* MYSHKIN*'s head reacting; after,* MYSHKIN *stares at* GANYA*:)*

MYSHKIN. That's all right for me, but not for Ippolit. He's thinking of writing something. *(breaks away into a corner)* Oh how ashamed you'll be! *(cries,* NATASHA *goes hesitantly to him)*

NATASHA. Prince –

MYSHKIN. And you – you know you're not really what you seem to be.

ROGOZHIN. *(grabs* GANYA*)* Natasha! *(She looks;* ROGOZHIN *says to* GANYA*:)* Slap me.

(GANYA *does; delay after slap before sound and his reaction.* ROGOZHIN *turns his other cheek.)*

Harder. Harder than you slapped him.

(GANYA *does, same delay but louder sound.)*

Oh, how ashamed you'll be!

(LEBEDEV *giggles;* GANYA *backs away, whimpering;* ROGOZHIN *to* NATASHA.*)*

And you – you know you're not really what you seem to be!! *(laughs)*

NATASHA. Very good, Rogozhin – stalemate!

ROGOZHIN. *(to* **MYSHKIN***)* Beware the good deed, Prince. Christianity has a way of worming into a woman's heart.

NATASHA. I'll decide whom to marry tonight! Rogozhin – perhaps a hundred thousand rubles would help me make up my mind!

LEBEDEV. A hundred thousand rubles!

ROGOZHIN. *(fingering the cross around* **MYSHKIN***'s neck)* Perhaps we'll meet again someday, Prince. *(to* **NATASHA***)* One hundred thousand rubles? One hundred thousand rubles .... *(snaps fingers at* **LEBEDEV***)* Come, my pet!

LEBEDEV. "Come, my pet!" Stick his head in your money pocket and pet obeys! Rowf, rowf! Good god! Good dog!

NATASHA. You must all come to my party tonight!

(all exit but **MYSHKIN***)*

MYSHKIN. When someone insults a Japanese, the Japanese goes up to him, takes out his knife – one of those curved things – and screams: "You have insulted me!" – whereupon he cuts his very own stomach out right before the insulter's eyes. I think it's Japanese – Japanese or Chinese. *(exits)*

*(MUSIC: **THE RUSSIAN GRUB JIG**. Party: **IVOGLINS** & **LEBEDEV**; **NATASHA** dancing, sings:)*

NATASHA.

2-4-6-8 MEN-MEN-MEN-MEN ALL TOUCH-AND-GO.

(with **GANYA***)*

HANDS UP MY DRESS? GROPING FOR KOPECKS?

(puts **GANYA***'s hands up her dress)*

GANYA, POOR GANYA, ALAS, I CONFESS:
THERE'S NOTHING UP THERE BUT MY ASS AND SOME SEX!

(Slaps his hands away, laughing; **MYSHKIN** *enters.)*

Well well well welcome, Prince!

MYSHKIN. Hello, Natasha Fillipovna.

NATASHA. Did life ever strike you as being deceptively good?

MYSHKIN. I find life perfectly normal. I've never had anything to compare it to.

NATASHA. *(laughing)* Then I must convert you, Prince! Say your prayers and I'll show you the best of evil around! Game time! Truth game – everyone must tell the worst thing he's ever done in his life! You'll be on your honor not to lie. Lebedev! *(She determines who speaks and for how long.)*

LEBEDEV. You're going to think I'm terrible – you'll say I'm awful – but I was young and foolish at the time and hadn't eaten in three days, so I went to the schoolyard, grabbed three small girls, took them home, raped them, slit their throats, cut them up, browned them, ate them, and threw their bones to the neighbors.

IPPOLIT. That's revolting!

GANYA. That's awful!

NATASHA. I'm sorry, Lebedev, you did nothing of the kind. I read that story in the newspaper this morning. Any more cheating and you're out of the game! *(points to* **GANYA***)*

GANYA. You mean besides masturbation and things like that?

LEBEDEV. I screwed a pig once – but that doesn't count.

IPPOLIT. The worst thing I ever did happened to me when I was five years old. I was bending over to pick up this toy and I felt the first tuberculosis germ taking its first bite into a cell in my lungs.

LEBEDEV. Sucking off swans, licking tongues with lambs!

NATASHA. Ganya!

GANYA. I remember the day well. The sun was out and there was sunlight. I was on a park bench that was painted some color. There was a tree or two – growing I imagine. There I was - awake, my mind working as it does when suddenly one of the most brilliant thoughts in the history of the human head, a though guaranteed to yield me riches beyond my dreams – this thought had just run though my…without me even knowing it. Something about mediocrity, I think.

LEBEDEV. Pounding nails into ears, sticking scorpions up your ass, and laughing at old ladies.

NATASHA. Those things don't shock us any more, Lebedev.

IVOGLIN. Ganya was thirteen, Ippolit was playing under the rug as he always did. My wife had just stabbed me in the shoulder with a meat knife. I had a terrible headache. The weather outside was awful. We were having tripe and turnips for dinner again. I was in a bad mood.

LEBEDEV. Sitting on babies' faces, sticking ear wax in your neighbor's beer, and pulling down your pants in front of grandma!

GANYA. There I was, making headway in recalling this thought, when a beggar began grabbing my attention. "Make your own living!" I yelled at him, and he…he … So I tried to get back to my thought, but all I could think of was: What if the beggar was really a rich man in disguise, waiting for someone to be kind to him, so he could repay the kindness with a big bag of money?

IVOGLIN. That was the day I did the worst thing in my life. I walked into a tavern and decided once and for all that imagination was a far far better thing than reality…As a matter of fact, I just made up this whole story!

NATASHA. Ippolit!

IPPOLIT. I felt that if I had never bent over in that one way to pick up that one toy, and had never breathed the particular breath of air I breathed at that moment in the particular way I breathed it, I would never have inflicted myself with tuberculosis. But I wasn't paying attention. I was careless. Haphazard.

NATASHA. Ganya!

GANYA. The thought of the disguised philanthropist kept pushing my brilliant thought further and further out of my … so finally, one night I trailed the bastard to his hut just to clear my head once and for all. I saw the beggar and his old wife drink themselves out of … and collapse on the floor, without even vomiting. And the whole night, peeking there through the window, I was wondering: Perhaps he knew I was shadowing him, so naturally he would keep up his beggar act. I didn't know what to think. And the worst thing is, of course…the worst thing…is…is

NATASHA. Lebedev.

LEBEDEV. Torturing idiots? …Lying about your childhood? Using bad language? *(kisses **MYSHKIN**)* Betraying your friends. Breast spit rectum Judas Priest and Christ Almighty!

NATASHA. *(laughing, stroking **LEBEDEV**)* Don't be ashamed, Lebedev – no one will remember those nasty things you've been saying when there's so much greater evil around. *(looks at **IPPOLIT**)*

LEBEDEV. I was just trying to pick up that cotton pigeon of mine that had stuffing coming out of its stomach. When I tugged at one of its eyes, I could see the little red threads holding it on. The stuffing didn't have any color. *(pause)*

NATASHA. Prince Myshkin…would you care to join my religion?

MYSHKIN. Oh no, please I have committed sins so evil, all of you are saints! No, I cannot tell you – you couldn't forgive me.

GANYA. Trust us. Trust us.

MYSHKIN. …Forgive me – I will. *(dramatic pause)* I once drank an entire glass of milk. *(puzzled reactions)* Not only that, but another time, I ruined an entire day sitting around waiting for my nose to clear up. Oh, I've committed sins! I've studied articles about utopia, sung love songs! I've created mucus and manufactured scabs. I've waltzed! Once I had an epileptic fit right in the middle of a dart game! *(The party is laughing now. To* **LEBEDEV***:)* Once I gave a lime to a child, and he started crying because it was so green. *(laughing)* Once I called God an idiot!

LEBEDEV. I used to steal Hosts and feed them to my puppy! And guess what! I write nursery rhymes! Look! *(pulls out a few scraps of paper and recites:)*
Uggy little buggies
get to live in ruggies;
goody goody goosie
hangs from a noosie.
I like little duckies.
I know I'm not that good, but –

IPPOLIT. That's nothing. I left my diary in a theater once, hoping someone would find it and make a play out of it!

IVOGLIN. Sometimes I drink in front of my children.

GANYA. *(to* **MYSHKIN***)* You should see me cheat at solitaire. *(laughs)*

NATASHA. Prince Myshkin … what is the worst thing I could do?

MYSHKIN. *(reluctantly)* I'm sorry.

NATASHA. Truth.

MYSHKIN. Marry Ganya.

GANYA. He wants the money for himself!

NATASHA. You'll get your money, Ganya.

GANYA. Why ask an idiot how to run your life?

NATASHA. *(sings:)*
THE GRUBS IN THE GARBAGE ARE WHITE.
THE BIRDS JUST FLAP AND DROP THEIR CRAP
AS THEY TWIT THEIR LITTLE DITTY –
OH SHIT, IT'S ALL SO PRETTY!
THE GRUBS IN THE GARBAGE SO WHI-ITE,

THE MEN OF OUR AGE SO FORTHRIGHT,
SO BRIGHT, SO PO-LITE, SO WHAT!!
YOU'RE THE PICK OF THE NOSE OF MANHOOD!
ONLY ONE MAN KNOWS IT'S NOT BAD TO BE GOOD,
SO GENTLE I WINCE,
SO UNGODLY HUMAN:
PRINCE M–

(**ROGOZHIN** *enters dramatically, with a wad of money.*)

LEBEDEV. *(ending song)* ROGOZHIN! ROGOZHIN!!

ROGOZHIN. *(throwing the wad at* **NATASHA***'s feet)* A hundred thousand birthdays, Natasha!

LEBEDEV. *(going for the money)* One hundred thousand!

ROGOZHIN. *(yanking* **LEBEDEV***)* Back! Back! Hurry, Natasha – take it!

NATASHA. Oh, please, Rogozhin – dramatics, dramatics, dramatics! Here, Ganya – would you like a wad? A little consolation prize? Here, poochie-poochie!

ROGOZHIN. Natasha, I would kill for you. I would kiss small children, I would carry packages for lepers, I would help you commit suicide – anything!

NATASHA. Wait your turn, Rogozhin, no dramatics. Now Ganya, I shall take these hundred thousand rubles and set fire to them. When they start burning, you may crawl to the fire. And then, using only your mouth, you may take as much money from the flames as you can stand. Ganya Ivoglin, ladies and gentlemen, at last face to face with pain exactly as greedy as he is! Here we go! *(She sets fire to the money and throws it in a glass bowl.)*

GANYA. Maybe if I proudly refuse to do whatever it is she wants me to do, she'll reward me with even greater money than I refuse! Maybe I'll grow wings and flap out of here and join a circus and make millions as the only flying rich man in the world!

LEBEDEV. Holy Christ, Natasha, it burns – one hundred thousand rubles is mortal!

GANYA. *(crawls to the fire)* If I had that money, I could stop smiling so much, buy a library of books about tuberculosis, contribute to the fire department, own a monocle, get an operation on my mouth, have money to burn ....

IVOGLIN. Fillipovna – I know families who live on no more than five or six grapes a day! That money –

GANYA. But I use my mouth! Helpful thoughts often creep into the world through my mouth! And if my head ever caught fire, how could I scream without my mouth? My mouth is almost worth a fortune to me! *(halts)*

IPPOLIT. That money could pay for a cure if I wanted to live.

GANYA. *(motionless to **MYSHKIN**)* You don't think I'm moving, do you? But in the head, still in the head socket, my thoughts are moving madly to maintain my immobility. I could sit here forever if you paid me enough. I could think here in my head for an eternity on whether to act or think here in my head for an eternity on whether to act or never make up my, my ... my ...

IPPOLIT. It could, Ganya, it could!

LEBEDEV. Ashes! A hundred thousand ashes!

*(**GANYA** realizes the money is gone, and slowly turns and crawls to the rocking chair, where he will barely rock, obliviously.)*

NATASHA. *(to **GANYA**, as he crawls)* Did you lose something, Ganya? Over here, Ganya – here I am. I've decided I will marry you after all.

*(**GANYA** doesn't hear. Though she addresses him, she's really aiming her remarks at **ROGOZHIN**.)*

But I must warn you – I gave away everything I own this morning. To a convent! That's right! *(laughs at **ROGOZHIN** 's reaction.)* Still no, Ganya? *(kisses **GANYA** 's blank forehead.)* Well, I think you've made the right decision. After all, I have nothing to offer. I want nothing. Who would have me now?

MYSHKIN. *(sings)*

    I'D HAVE YOU.
    YOU NEED TO BE TAKEN CARE OF.
    I'D HONOR, RESPECT AND WAIT ON YOU.
    I'D GIVE YOU –
    ALL –
    MY LOVE.

    IF WE SHOULD BE POOR, I'D WORK FOR YOU.
    YOU'D SUFFER NO MORE – WE'D EAT STEW.

    BUT –
    WE WON'T BE POOR.
    OUR LOVE WILL MAKE US RICH!
    BESIDES I BELIEVE I'M A ROYAL INHERITOR!
    OR SO SAYS THIS LETTER –
    FROM THE DUKE OF MACKAVITCH....

    *(**LEBEDEV** grabs the letter, reads it.)*

NATASHA. *(embracing **MYSHKIN**)* Prince! I'll be your princess! I shall impose tariffs! Prince! We shall rule the stew and read children's stories. We shall come true. *(**MYSHKIN** is cold, confused, stares at **ROGOZHIN**.)* Off with his head!!

ROGOZHIN. *(to **MYSHKIN**)* Spastic virgin! Why should I kill you?

LEBEDEV. *(reading letter)* Twenty rubles ev'ry winter?! That's it?! *(returns letter)* Great inheritance, Prince!

MYSHKIN. *(offering letter to **IPPOLIT**)* It's not much, Ippolit, but you can start saving for a cure.

ROGOZHIN. *(grabs letter)* Beware the good deed, Prince. I burn your charity.... *(burns the letter; **IPPOLIT** protests)* And I take these black ashes *(from the burnt rubles)* and change them into ... a hundred thousand rubles! *(It appears he does.)*

MYSHKIN. How did you do that?

ROGOZHIN. *(giving the wad to **IPPOLIT**)* To your health, Ippolit. And now I take Natasha Fillipovna and turn her into...my wife!

MYSHKIN. *(still referring to the magic trick)* How did you do that?

ROGOZHIN. I forgive you.

NATASHA. Goodbye, Prince. You're very silly. You're the best person I've ever met. Marry the noncontroversial Aglaya Yepanchin. You're too good for me...too bad for you!

(She runs off laughing with **ROGOZHIN**, *followed apostolically by* **LEBEDEV**.*)*

IPPOLIT. *(calling after them, waving the money)* Thank you very much!

MYSHKIN. *(examining the money)* This money's counterfeit!

(Bass: thump, thump, thump... **IPPOLIT** *begins a big coughing fit.* **IVOGLIN** *helps him and* **GANYA** *off.* **MYSHKIN**, *alone, calls after:)*

Is there anything I can say? ...I never say what I want to say. Like a god continually chattering about atheism! I don't understand – I am subject to epilepsy.

*(***MYSHKIN*** is outside, fitful. He feels ***ROGOZHIN****'s eyes on him. Are there* **CROWDPEOPLE** *milling neuterly about him, or are they offstage?* **NATASHA** *runs up to him frantically. Her hair is down.)*

NATASHA. I was supposed to marry Rogozhin again tody. But I ditched him. He bored me. Bored me black and blue. Beat me stiff. To tears! Eyes! Eyes!

(She runs off. **CROWDPEOPLE CHORUS** *sings* FITTING *as* **ROGOZHIN** *shadows the haunted* **MYSHKIN***:)*

CHORUS.
EYES
LIKE HANDCUFFS
SHADOWING YOU,
CERTAIN NERVE ENDS SPLITTING –
IT'S ALL SO FITTING,
FITTING!
IT'S ALL SO ...
SO ...

NOW WHERE DID THOSE WORDS GO?
WHERE DID I PUT THAT THOUGHT?
SIMPLE, SIMPLE:
I FORGOT ....

(Music & CHORUS *out;* MYSHKIN *at* ROGOZHIN*'s opened door.)*

ROGOZHIN. How did you know this was my house?

MYSHKIN. The grass in front...the way the tree... *(demonstrates how the tree looked)* Is Natasha –

ROGOZHIN. Last night she made me chain her to the staircase. She was afraid she'd run off to you again like she does on all our wedding days. This morning she was gone.

MYSHKIN. Stand there. Stare at me. Use your eyes. *(tests the stare with his back)* You were following me today I think.

ROGOZHIN. You are insane.

MYSHKIN. I don't think he is. Nobody is. Of course they are, but – I'm sorry – I'm...today I am...distracted... I feel the way I used to before my fits. *(looks around)* Natasha?

ROGOZHIN. But she'll come back sometime tonight, just to bitch at me about how she's loved you since that birthday party of hers. And how she'll go insane if she doesn't figure out whether to love you like her father or like her own child. I'll grind my teeth and think of you with dust in my mouth.

MYSHKIN. Natasha must leave St. Petersburg! Her head's a party! No music left. Too large a crowd.... One more puff of cigar smoke: poof. *(*ROGOZHIN *laughs loudly.)* She gags to death on fun. I'm very fond of you, Paryfon.

ROGOZHIN. What?

MYSHKIN. I'm very fond of you, Paryfon, even though I'm sure you haven't laughed correctly in years. If you refuse to scream at me, I can do no good here. ...I'm leaving. I'll see you in heaven. Goodbye.

ROGOZHIN. *(screaming)* PLEASE STAY!! When you're not right here, right before me, I hate you. I don't eat, I don't move, I don't put my clothes on. I'm so busy deciding whether I should poison you, use the knife, acid – but what kind of poison? Setting fire to your bed? Naw. How about those sucking things…?

MYSHKIN. Lampreys?

ROGOZHIN. No, wouldn't work. Probably poison – but what kind? (**MYSHKIN** *is playing with the knife.*) You see? When you're not here? But here you are …

MYSHKIN. *(indicating knife)* Is this new?

ROGOZHIN. *(grabbing it away)* WHY AM I SCREAMING AT YOU?! …Her in bed, me sleeping in the closet. I hear her fall out of bed…

(**NATASHA** *falls out onto stage, acts out the scene as described.*)

– gets on her knees, mumbling and moaning –

NATASHA. Oh my Prince, forgive me, I cannot marry you. If I should die before I wake –

ROGOZHIN. *(in the scene with* **NATASHA** *now, beating her)* Prince! Prince! Prince! *(to* **MYSHKIN***)* And I beat her in your name. Then I'm wretched for days afterwards. She brings armies inn – zookeepers, judges! – then she throws me a biscuit in front of them. I sit there. I don't move until she talks to me again. Once it was three days.

NATASHA. *(to* **ROGOZHIN***)* What are you thinking?

ROGOZHIN. The way your legs go all the way up to the bottom of your stomach.

NATASHA. The way you beat me?

ROGOZHIN. The way your teeth show when you yawn.

NATASHA. I'll marry you, Paryfon. *(yawning)* See my teeth?

(*As* **ROGOZHIN & NATASHA** *start making love,* **MYSHKIN** *tentatively approaches them like a wondering child, and the* **CHORUS** *re-enters:*)

CHORUS. *(singing)*
> THERE'S JUST ONE THING –
> FITTING NOW,
> FITTING –

> *(converging neuterly on* **MYSHKIN,** *who stars toying
> with* **ROGOZHIN** *'s knife)*

> THERE'S A DAGGER
> WITH A BLADE
> WITH A HANDLE
> WITH A HAND –

> SIMPLE, SIMPLE:
> I STAGGER
> I BLEED
> I CANNOT STAND ....

> **(CHORUS** *is off, music fades.* **NATASHA** *vanishes, and*
> **ROGOZHIN** *grabs the knife from* **MYSHKIN.** *)*

ROGOZHIN. Godammit, leave that alone!

MYSHKIN. It is new, isn't it?

ROGOZHIN. Can't I buy a letter opener if I want?

MYSHKIN. *(smelling* **ROGOZHIN** *'s hand)* Natasha? She needs
rest, peace. Oceans crushing rock. You'll kill her. I forgive you. It is new. What is that picture? But that really
is Christ on the cross! Is it an early photograph?

*(***ROGOZHIN*** laughs.* ***MYSHKIN*** laughs and strikes a
pose in imitation of the picture.)*

Ugly. He'll die in one minute. A person could lose his
faith looking at that picture. In one minute.

ROGOZHIN. That's what Natasha sees in you, Prince…Tell
me about God.

MYSHKIN. With words? The eyes?

ROGOZHIN. What eyes?

MYSHKIN. That we get seeing from? *(pointing to his eyes)*
Behind these. God of the brain cell? *(holding head)*
Here's infinity. More thoughts in this room than atoms
in the universe! In just these last five seconds, Paryfon,

you've seen this hand *(moving his hand; footsteps are heard)* – move every millionth of an inch from here … to here.

*(**CROWDPEOPLE CHORUS** marches in a line between the staring **MYSHKIN** and **ROGOZHIN**.)*

IVOGLIN. You've known the color of my trousers –

MME. YEPANCHIN. – whether you've known it or not.

IPPOLIT. You've been thinking under your breath:

NATASHA. Does Natasha think he's handsome?

GANYA. Who are we?

AGLAYA. He's a fool!

LEBEDEV. I'm getting hungry.

*(The **CHORUS** has marched out.)*

MYSHKIN. …and shall you kill me. And for some ungodly reason you were thinking of – gerbils? Those little rodents?

ROGOZHIN. Right.

MYSHKIN. - and over all that you were listening to me! How can all those big thoughts fit in a little head like yours? Where do they go? God takes them.

ROGOZHIN. *(pointing to the cross around **MYSHKIN**'s neck)* What's that cross?

MYSHKIN. Tin.

ROGOZHIN. *(taking gold cross from his own neck)* Solid gold. We'll exchange. *(**MYSHKIN** hesitates.)* It will make us brothers.

MYSHKIN. God bless you, brother Paryfon.

*(The exchange is made. **ROGOZHIN** kisses **MYSHKIN** on the mouth. Pause.)*

ROGOZHIN. My mother shall bless you. Come.

*(Music. **ROGOZHIN** guides **MYSHKIN** through a maze to a **HEADLESS OLD HEAP**, who begin chanting and blessing **MYSHKIN** with its crippled hand as soon as they enter her space.)*

ROGOZHIN. Mother, this is Prince Myshkin. We have exchanged crosses and become brothers. Could you give him your blessing, you old hag – straight from the scales of your boney womb? You're like death stinking up my house and rotting out my floors! You'd better die soon, or I'll snap you apart and build a cabinet out of you! Ha! Ha-ha-ha! (**MYSHKIN** *is confused.*) She's blind and completely deaf. I'm always teasing her. She's not even my mother – I just found her here. But that was something … she knew you were there, and she knew I wanted you blessed!

(*Rips the shawl off the* **HEADLESS OLD HEAP**, *revealing the giggling* **LEBEDEV**. **MYSHKIN**, *stunned, begins wandering away.*)

LEBEDEV. He didn't tell me how shaky you were!

(**ROGOZHIN** *leads the dazed* **MYSHKIN** *out.*)

ROGOZHIN. No, no – this way, this way ….

CHORUS. (*entering, singing:*)
EAGLES SCREAM AND BULLS GIVE BIRTH …

MYSHKIN. I've forgotten … haven't I forgotten something?

CHORUS.
MARS DEAD FROM THE SMELL OF EARTH …

ROGOZHIN. Go, babyface! Natasha is yours – take her then!

CHORUS.
WORMS IN WORSHIP OF THE DUST
BLOODY KNIVES TURN TO RUST …

MYSHKIN. I've forgotten something!

CHORUS.
FITTING, FITTING …

MYSHKIN. I think I've forgotten something!

CHORUS.
FITS –

ROGOZHIN. Remember Rogozhin! (*pushes him out*)

CHORUS WOMAN. (*whispering*)
FIT!

*(**MYSHKIN** leaves the house. The **CROWDPEOPLE** form a tableau around him. **ROGOZHIN** is somewhere staring at him.)*

MYSHKIN. I must forget something … I can't remember – what? Like a donkey. Life! Something to do with life …. eyes!!

(wheels around suddenly, looking for the staring eyes; freezes in his wheel around position; tests the position)

This is a nice position. Myshkin – discus thrower! Myshkin, as he was at one moment in the history of history and always will have been from here on on! Note the straining tendons in the neck, the sinewy arms uplifted, the heart like a kettle drum finishing off a symphony! Over here, fellow art lovers, we have the marvelous life-like statue entitled: "Prekinetic Man in Crescendoing Stasis!" Myshkin – gathering up all his life forces before … total action! Myshkin – acting like an idiot! *(breaks the freeze)* Playing! Idiot! Wasting God! … Ah. Coming now One thought. The one thought. The one thought that means – everything! Sh ….

*(MUSIC: **FITTING**.)*

CROWDPERSON 1. The aura is the pause just before the seizure, in which the epileptic experiences an extraordinary intensification of self-awareness and an extreme consciousness of existence.

MYSHKIN. Noblest feeling alive, highest extant experience–

CROWDPERSON 2. – followed immediately, inseparably, by the ignobility of the ridiculous fit –

MYSHKIN. – trying to get rid of my body –

CROWDPERSON 3. as if being punished for overhearing God's secret formula–

*(**ROGOZHIN** is still staring.)*

MYSHKIN. –for being stared at so intensely by two cosmic eyes, suddenly seeing the fire they're made of, brilliant colorless fire, constantly burning through every impulse in the universe!

CROWDPERSON 4. And you have stolen one thin flame of the fire, and you must relive all of Prometheus's life in the next ten seconds –

MYSHKIN. – those two eyes of fire at the top of these stairs–

*(***NATASHA****'s stairs – She is standing serenely at the top;* **ROGOZHIN** *crouches with his knife out.)*

I will tell Natasha the secret; the one thought over all and under all: life is everything! I am worth an infinity of thought and there is something greater than me, two eyes that have been following me ever since I can remember! … Whatever happens, whatever idiocy – for this radiant moment I would give my entire life –

*(***ROGOZHIN** *leaps out from the stairwell with knife raised.* **NATASHA** *silent at the top of stairs. MUSIC up;* **ROGOZHIN** *freezes.* **MYSHKIN** *sings a song:)*

I SEE THROUGH THE EYES WATCHING OVER ME:
I'M ALIVE BEYOND ALL ILLUSION!
AND EACH MOMENT OF LIFE KNOWS AN ECSTACY
BURIED WITHIN OUR CONFUSION.

*(***MYSHKIN** *&* **CHORUS** *sing simultaneously:)*

MYSHKIN.	**CHORUS.**
I SEE THROUGH THE EYES WATCHING OVER ME	EAGLES SCREAM AND BULLS GIVE BIRTH –
I'M ALIVE BEYOND ALL ILLUSION,	MARS DEAD FROM THE SMELL OF EARTH –
AND EACH MOMENT OF LIFE KNOWS AN ECSTASY	WORMS IN WORSHIP OF THE DUST –
BURIED WITHIN OUR CONFUSION -	BLOODY KNIVES TURN TO RUST-

(On the word "confusion," **MYSHKIN** *begins his epileptic scream and returns to the murder situation –* **ROGOZHIN** *raising his knife. The scream and fit frighten* **ROGOZHIN** *from murder.* **MYSHKIN** *falls down the stairs.)*

CHORUS.
 FITTING! FITTING!
 FITS!
 FIT!

 (**MYSHKIN** *a rigid quiver. Blackout. End of Act I*)

ACT II

*(**MYSHKIN** is prostrate, as he was at the end of Act I, after his fit. He slowly raises his head.)*

MYSHKIN. Today is my birthday.

*(With a scream, **IPPOLIT** appears and crawls to **MYSHKIN**.)*

IPPOLIT. I had a nightmare about you, Prince. I dreamed you had an epileptic fit and fell down a staircase. I crawled over to you and you looked at me so kindly, your forehead cracked. I put my hands through the crack, around your brain, and truer than tuberculosis you told me:

MYSHKIN. You are going to die, Ippolit. I understand.

IPPOLIT. How should I die then, Prince?

MYSHKIN. Leave us your life, and forgive us our happiness.

IPPOLIT. That's what you said in the dream!

*(Exits; **MYSHKIN** starts writing letters.*

*Enter **ROGOZHIN** and **LEBEDEV**.)*

ROGOZHIN. Does he suspect I'm paying you to keep him at your house?

LEBEDEV. How should I know? All we ever talk about's my childhood.

ROGOZHIN. *(paying **LEBEDEV**)* Find out who he's writing those letters to.

LEBEDEV. *(as he exits with **ROGOZHIN**)* I really hate my childhood!

*(**MME. YEPANCHIN** visits **MYSHKIN**.)*

MME. YEPANCHIN. *(knitting)* Now, Prince – did you or did you not send Aglaya a letter this morning?

MYSHKIN. Yes. An enormous upsurge of happiness had completely dispirited me. The sun was over there. Tomorrow is my birthday. I was silent. So I wrote Aglaya, yes.

MME. YEPANCHIN. This letter, did it concern you and Aglaya having a … relationship.

MYSHKIN. That's all we have. Here. I'll recite it by heart. *(pointing to his head)* Anything I add here, stays.

AGLAYA. *(entering, reading the letter)* "To the living Aglaya. I am writing you this. How is it that I am? I pray, remember myself to you and together as it happens we are brought to mind. I have no particular words to write. Please be reading this now. I am, your brother, Prince Lyov Myshkin."

(She looks up, puzzled.)

MME. YEPANCHIN. Ah me – human relationships befuddle me so. Everyone has them.

MYSHKIN. Women think so highly of me.

MME. YEPANCHIN. I love the Bible. I love falling asleep. I love saying things. That's how I love you, Prince. Aglaya, however, loves you precisely the same way, only in a younger manner. It's a goodly love, Prince, a very goodly love. But it's not the same love God uses to populate the earth.

(She sticks the knitting needle firmly into the ball of yarn and holds the sweater up against **MYSHKIN** *to see how it fits.* **AGLAYA** *comes up to* **MYSHKIN**:*)*

AGLAYA. I got your love letter.

MYSHKIN. Love– ? On no – I assure you, I only sent that letter from the depths of my soul. I –

AGLAYA. You must run away with me. You're perfect. So am I. We're perfect for each other. You're the only reality on earth. I've never seen a single Gothic cathedral.

MYSHKIN. This is absurd, Aglaya!

AGLAYA. Do you think I'd run off with an idiot like you?!

(leaves in a huff)

MME. YEPANCHIN. *(disappointed with the fit of the sweater)* Aglaya's just like me and it worries me sick. We really don't fit our society, Prince, but for the greater honor and glory of God, we try. *(sighs, puts away knitting, prepares to leave)* God's a bit of a misfit himself. We should all be put in glass cages for display. Well – I'd best leave you to your thoughts.

(She bustles off.

AGLAYA *returns when* **MME. YEPANCHIN** *is gone.)*

AGLAYA. I am being kept in a glass cage! You must run away with me! I can't even bear to look at you! Your eyes are kind. Your whole head is ugly! Natasha Fillipovna wrote me this letter.

*(***NATASHA*** *appears, writing a letter. As* **MYSHKIN** *reads the letter silently,* **NATASHA** *reads what she writes:)*

NATASHA. "Aglaya, Aglaya – I can imagine your golden body under your fine tight clothes screaming to be free. I am on fire for you. You and the Prince must marry."

*(***ROGOZHIN*** *enters* **NATASHA***'s area and looks over her shoulder;* **AGLAYA** *is looking over* **MYSHKIN***'s shoulder.)*

NATASHA & MYSHKIN. *(reading the same part of the letter in their respective areas)* "I think of you both as inseparable as two burning eyes, as silver knife and golden sheath."

ROGOZHIN. *(reading over* **NATASHA***'s shoulder)* "Roggy just laughed at what I wrote. I will marry him only when you marry the Prince."

NATASHA. "P.S., he hides his knife in the cobwebs of his mother's bedpan."

NATASHA & AGLAYA. "By the end of your honeymoon, my blood will be gray. I will be dying at your defloration. Do not think of me."

(All pause to turn the letters over in unison.)

AGLAYA. "Marry Myshkin! He is the resurrection! Hurry! The rats are eating something under the floor. Keep the commandments. All my love," signed –

MYSHKIN. "Natasha Fillipovna!"

(**AGLAYA** *runs off.* **NATASHA** *laughs.*)

NATASHA. *(to* **ROGOZHIN***)* The little bitch! She has moles on her ass. Why don't you kill me before I write her another letter. Oh dear, Paryfon. You must do something for me. Ever since the Prince's fit I've been having these long periods of happiness I can't seem to snap myself out of. I've taken to sitting in trees with children and making up words with them. I spend an hour eating an olive. I help strangers rake their leaves. I believe in God, the Prince will marry Aglaya, I think about giraffes! I can't stand it, Paryfon – I'm going to go pick a rose.

ROGOZHIN. You're not convincing, Natasha.

NATASHA. He's fallen in love with you.

(*She runs off;* **ROGOZHIN** *turns and is startled to confront:* **MYSHKIN**. *Silence. Then:*)

ROGOZHIN. You know that letter you sent me – well, I burned it! Did it say you forgave me?

MYSHKIN. Remember? You tried to murder me. I had a fit. You –

ROGOZHIN. Of course I remember! How could I forget? You scared me half to death! The letter – did it say you forgave me, that we were still brothers, and that evil is not the worst thing in the world?

MYSHKIN. No, it didn't. I was merely inquiring if I had left my hat at your house that day we exchanged crosses.

ROGOZHIN. I didn't steal your hat!

MYSHKIN. Paryfon, we're brothers! Evil is not the worst thing in the world.

ROGOZHIN. What is?

MYSHKIN. Loneliness.

(**NATASHA**, *with a rose, has crawled to* **MYSHKIN**'s *feet and is kissing them, humming and laughing.*)

Natasha! Get up, please – must I dig a hole to show you my position with respect to you.

NATASHA. Then I should dig a deeper hole.

MYSHKIN. And I a deeper.

NATASHA. I am unworthy to dig holes at your feet!

ROGOZHIN. Oh God!

(He drags laughing NATASHA away. MYSHKIN calls after them:)

MYSHKIN. Today is my birthday!

IPPOLIT, GANYA, LEBEDEV, MME. YEPANCHIN & AGLAYA. *(appearing)* HAPPY BIRTHDAY!!!

MME. YEPANCHIN. *(holding a sweater up to him)* Oh, my goodness, Prince, you still don't fit!

LEBEDEV. Here's a present that came for you in the mail. It's signed, "from your brother."

(He places the too small hat on MYSHKIN's head.)

MME. YEPANCHIN. Oh, Prince, I swear, your head must grow a pound a day.

MYSHKIN. Hello, Aglaya.

AGLAYA. Ganya, where's your father?

GANYA. He had a stroke telling lies to the prince.

IPPOLIT. *(with notebook)* Prince! I have written something for your birthday! Please! Everyone sit! It's my life story. It'll only take three minutes.

GANYA. Three minutes! For your life? An eternity in mine!

MME. YEPANCHIN. Ganya Ivoglin!

GANYA. Well, what if it's boring? What do I do with the inside of my head in the meantime? An eternity!

MYSHKIN. Ippolit! *(starts applauding; applause)*

IPPOLIT. *(reading)* "The Summation and Conclusion of My Life, by Ippolit Ivoglin – *(applause)* – A Consumptive in His Last Agonies."

LEBEDEV. I hope it's dirty!

IPPOLIT. "Roman numeral eye: LIFE –"

GANYA. Life?! *(starts laughing loudly)*

IPPOLIT. There are about four things in life not even you can laugh at, Ganya. *(hawks and spits)* That's one of them.

(**LEBEDEV** *wearily gets dustpan and broom.*)

GANYA. That's quite unnecessary, you know.

IPPOLIT. Unnecessary, thoughtless, and no reason for it all – yet there it is! It's puce! *(hawks again)* Seems to be no end to the little buggers, does there?

LEBEDEV. *(sweeping up the two blobs)* Every time you come over here you have to show off your tuberculosis!

MYSHKIN. IPPOLIT! *(begins applause again)*

IPPOLIT. *(reading:)* Prince Myshkin says: "It is memory that decides what we have left of our lives at death. Act memorably, and you'll die with a fuller life left you."

(Applause. The women nod appreciatively to **MYSHKIN.***)*

Roman number eye-eye: MY LIFE, THE LIFE LEFT ME: My only two memorable memories. One – when I was first learning to read, discovering the word "eye." Small e, small y, small e. It made a face, the look of that word.

Memory two. When I was twelve and the wind blew a button off Katerina Petrovna's blouse and for two entire seconds I saw her actual breast and a real nipple issuing from the one end of it. Unwrinkled. Not a toothmark on it. And it all looked so hard and so soft and so naturally there that I coughed five straight minutes without breathing once. *(laughter)* And scattered other memories – including: potato soup, one or two thoughts I've had in my life. Gerbil puppies. And the joke about what the ant colony said to the prostitute. That's the life left me. Everything else is covered with tuberculosis. Roman numeral eye-eye-eye: MY ULTIMATE CONCLUSION.

GANYA. At last!

IPPOLIT. I have a small pistol. After I am done reading this, as the sun sets, I shall shoot myself in the chest as many times as possible. Suicide is the only worthwhile project

I have time to begin and conclude of my own free will. It is the only cure known for terminal tuberculosis. It is a solid kick in the crotch of God. It is my ultimate conclusion. Roman numeral eye–eye–eye–eye–

GANYA. Oh my God, there's more!

IPPOLIT. MY LAST STATEMENT! No one can ever express all of what he wants to express. Everyone will die without communicating an essence to a single soul. And finally – *(pushing through* **GANYA***'s groans)* Roman numeral eye-eye-eye-eye-eye: THE ULTIMATE QUESTION. Is it worthwhile living when you know you're definitely going to die…within a hundred years? THE END.

MME. YEPANCHIN. *(applauding, going quickly to* **IPPOLIT***)* Young man, I came to this party hoping to help Prince Myshkin recover from his last fit. Obviously, I was disappointed. You would provide a more than welcome substitute. *(The sweater seems to be* **IPPOLIT***'s size.)* I do not find you pitiful. I enjoy helping people die with less despair. It clears my sinuses. It helps me live longer. If you would come live with us, both you and I would be eternally grateful.

IPPOLIT. *(to* **MYSHKIN***)* Goodbye, Prince. I only wish I had as much time for you as they do.

(He pulls out his small pistol and runs upstairs; Everyone runs after him.)

MYSHKIN. IPPOLIT!!

(Freeze - **IPPOLIT** *with his gun at his chest.*

MYSHKIN *goes to a flashback scene with* **IVOGLIN***.)*

IVOGLIN. Come back in time with me, Prince. It's been a long life, a tall tall tale of spicy wine, and I have some corking memories for my living – because I didn't miss a drop of it. But - I must confess everything to you, Prince – I could never have done it without Napoleon's personal help.

MYSHKIN. How did you and Napoleon meet, General?

IVOGLIN. Ah, Prince – my greatest memory, my *raison d'être*, as Napoleon's troops used to say! I shouldn't tell you, Prince – it's too exciting! *(clutches his heart)*

MYSHKIN. Ahh, *mon Génerál – pourquoi?*

IVOGLIN. *(laughing) Eh bien!* It's a tiny story, Prince, but so is life, non?

(Party scene unfreezes; AGLAYA *screams.)*

LEBEDEV. He wasn't lying!

*(*IPPOLIT *is motionless, gun at chest.)*

GANYA. Don't move! You might scare him!

LEBEDEV. I'll be goddamned if I'm cleaning up that mess!

(party scene freezes)

IVOGLIN. The night before I captured Napoleon, I slept in a marsh and a tiny childlike spider crawled up my nose and onto my braincase, making it impossible for me to sleep. And so, disgruntled and unshaven, I rose and plodded on.

IPPOLIT. *(immobile, in his head)* There should be one perfect last thought – God, don't let me waste this moment letting my mind wander … Aglaya is pretty. Lively.

IVOGLIN. Right before dawn, I captured Napoleon overconfidently relieving himself into the thundering rapids outside the ken of his campsite. I had just convinced him to retreat from Moscow when seventeen guards suddenly jumped me! "La guillotine!" Napoleon commanded.

MYSHKIN. The guillotine! I know the guillotine!

IVOGLIN. As they prepared the blade, one thought kept running through my head – alongside my spider.

MYSHKIN. I know! I know! You were thinking: "What if I had more than one minute to live!" Non? Non?

IVOGLIN. *Oui! Oui!*

IPPOLIT. Thirteen seconds, the sun will set – perhaps I should do it tomorrow. One more day can't hurt! Twelve seconds.

GANYA. No one move – if we wait long enough, he'll have a coughing fit.

IVOGLIN. And – "What if I had five more minutes? Or imagine – a lifetime!" Ha-ha! Oh, Prince – this story… *(breathing hard, clutching his heart)*

MYSHKIN. Go on, General, finish!

IPPOLIT. There very well might be an afterlife. Last thought, last thought…I'm hungry.

IVOGLIN. Well… *(gulping a drink, panting)* Just as the executioner raised his arm, the tiny childlike spider fell out of my nose and Napoleon saw me smile at it! "Cessez," Napoleon cried, and ran to me, weeping: "You are free, cher Génerál, because I have seen your love for life!" And the sun rose!!

IPPOLIT. The sunset!! *(pulls the trigger; no shot; empty clicks)*

IVOGLIN. "We all know, *théoriquement*," Napoleon went on, "that we must die someday – but now you are one of the only living people on earth who truly understands this beautiful inevitability."

GANYA. *(taking the gun from **IPPOLIT**)* Ohhh he "forgot" to put the firing caps in! Ha-ha! *(laughter)*

IPPOLIT. Give me my gun back!!

*(The party exits. **IPPOLIT** is coughing heavily. **MYSHKIN** vacillates between **IPPOLIT** and **IVOGLIN**.)*

IVOGLIN. "You have an eternity left to live! Go! And don't miss a moment!" And to this day I have followed Napoleon's advice as loyally as his troops followed him from Moscow.

IPPOLIT. Understand, Prince: I refuse to live a life that can assume such laughable, grotesque forms.

(has a coughing fit and faints)

IVOGLIN. Ah, Prince, I wish you had been there. Sometimes I feel very sorry for you, Prince. I find I have nothing more to say. I've said nothing. I never met Napoleon. Oh, we exchanged a few letters…now and then…but – what else is there to talk about then? How's life? Things? Dull, factual forms. I am not having a stroke!

(He has a stroke.)

MYSHKIN. *(between the two prostrate bodies)* I know…what the chopped head was thinking.

*(Lights dim. **NATASHA** wafts by, singing to him:)*

NATASHA.

STARE AT THE SUN,
FIT SOME FIRE IN YOUR EYES.
HEAR OUT THE SOUND
OF A CHOIR OF FLIES.

*(sings to **ROGOZHIN**, revealed in the darkness:)*

SLEEP DEEP IN THE EARTH,
PLAY GRAVE IN THE GROUND

(going off)

SEIZE YOUR –
SEIZE YOUR BIRTH.

(gone)

ROGOZHIN. Are you happy? …Natasha wants to know.

MYSHKIN. Oh no no no no no. She mustn't worry – there's no need for me to be happy.

ROGOZHIN. Lyov, I want to celebrate your birthday. We'll play death.

MYSHKIN. *(laughing)* Oh yes, yes, Paryfon, I'd like that. I've been much too serious lately. How do we play? *(laughing)* I've forgotten – it's been such a long time.

ROGOZHIN. This way, this way …

*(**ROGOZHIN** leads **MYSHKIN** to a freshly dug grave. **NATASHA** hums "Seizure" in the distance.)*

ROGOZHIN. Happy birthday!

MYSHKIN. *(delighted)* A long hole!

ROGOZHIN. Do you like it. I just dug it tonight. It's new. *(hands **MYSHKIN** some dirt)* Smell.

MYSHKIN. *(smells)* Old brain molecules. Worms have recently held services here. *(laughs)* Oh Paryfon, I'm so glad I'm not someone else! What now?

ROGOZHIN. *(pointing to the hole)* We lie.

(The two descend into the grave and lie side by side. Suppressed laughter. Pause.)

ROGOZHIN. We are dead.

MYSHKIN. Yes, yes - I'm remembering now. This is how it all started.

ROGOZHIN. Our heads begin leaking. Silk worms grub after our memory materials. Our brain cells turn to salt water and all our gods trickle out into one another.

MYSHKIN. Paryfon Rogozhin. *(laughs)* It's scary the way I laugh sometimes.

ROGOZHIN. Prince…sometimes beating Natasha and ter-rifying people and destroying myself – sometimes I get in moods where it all seems so empty and meaning-less. I try thinking of hurricanes, vivisection, talking behind people's backs – but nothing seems to inspire me until I think of your sympathy, your brainsucking. That's death, Prince, and I envy you that.

MYSHKIN. If only you could have a seizure with me.

ROGOZHIN. *(laughs)* I should strangle you. Real death, not just talk.

*(**MYSHKIN** holds up his hand.)*

MYSHKIN. This hand scares you more than death.

*(He places it over **ROGOZHIN**'s heart. Stillness. **NATASHA** is heard humming.)*

ROGOZHIN. My heart!

MYSHKIN. Ssh. It's all right.

ROGOZHIN. It is not! I may be dying!

MYSHKIN. You're not.

*(**ROGOZHIN** gasps, then presses **MYSHKIN**'s hand with both his hands.*

***NATASHA** enters with a rose.)*

NATASHA. Stop it! STOP! *(She pulls* **ROGOZHIN** *away; to* **MYSHKIN**:*)* Marry Aglaya. *(She grabs the rose stem, pulls her hand down it, gasps as her hand bleeds and hands the rose to* **MYSHKIN**.*)* No thorns on her.

(**ROGOZHIN** *pulls* **NATASHA** *away.* **AGLAYA** *rises from the grave and sings to* **MYSHKIN**:*)*

AGLAYA.

BEHOLD THE CHILD!
DYING FOR REBIRTH,
CRYING FOR DELIVERY.
BUT WE'RE OUT OF WOMBS, CHILD,
ALL OVER THE EARTH,
WE'RE ALL ALL OUT OF OLD OLD WOMBS –

ENTER A NEW WOMB WITH ME, CHILD.
WE'LL TALK AND WE'LL HIDE
AS THE WORLD ENDS OUTSIDE ....

PICK ME FIVE GREEN LEAVES FROM THE REDWOOD TREE
AND I WILL SPEAK THE FIRST WORDS OF MY LIFE.
DUMP TWELVE MILLION BABIES
IN THE DEEP GREEN SEA
AND TAKE ME FOR YOUR WIFE.

(**MYSHKIN** *gives her the rose.*)

MYSHKIN. You don't terrify me the same way Natasha does.

AGLAYA. We'll play chess. *(setting the board before him)* Your move. (**MYSHKIN** *stares dumbly as* **AGLAYA** *reaches over and makes a definite move.)* Mate!! Ha ha ha! You move as if you've never played before.

MYSHKIN. I haven't.

AGLAYA. Then how do you know how to move at all?

MYSHKIN. I read your mind.

AGLAYA. Ha ha! We'll play another. My move – mate. Ha-ha-ha! I win another! You're awful! Ha-ha! Do you know how to play "Fools?"

MYSHKIN. The card game? Why, yes! In fact, I've won several medals in various "Fools" tournaments. Isn't it funny how that it so? I mean, with people so dedicated to the idea that I'm a fool myself

AGLAYA. Yes, very funny. Perhaps we should call it "Idiots" instead! Or "Ninnies!" Hee-haw – your play, donkey-ears.

MYSHKIN. *(slapping down his cards triumphantly)* Fools, fools, fools, double-fools, crazy card and fools!! … Frightening, isn't it? I believe I play this game flawlessly. Another?

AGLAYA. *(lays down a card, hiding others under her foot)* Joker.

MYSHKIN. Trump jack, club-over, fools, nits, and underbogey! Three fools – my game! …You should've hidden the *other* dummy set under your foot.

AGLAYA. *(getting angrier)* Your deal! Three's up, double dunce.

MYSHKIN. Triple nits!

AGLAYA. Four open, over yours.

MYSHKIN. Under yours.

AGLAYA. Madcap.

MYSHKIN. Rummy!

AGLAYA. Joker!!

MYSHKIN. Fool!!!! Ha-ha …I mean fools! You see? This game? Sometimes I can hardly believe I'm so good – a virtual master.

AGLAYA. You ought to be ashamed visiting this house after running around with that Fillipovna woman. Get out!! (**MYSHKIN** *slumps off.*) Maman!

MME. YEPANCHIN. *(entering)* Where's the Prince?

AGLAYA. *(putting her game away; discovers a stuffed gerbil)* He had to go. Where's Ippolit?

MME. YEPANCHIN. Over there.

(**AGLAYA** *goes to* **IPPOLIT.**)

Either there's a bad smell of love in the air, or the cook put chocolate in the gravy again.

AGLAYA. Dear Ippolit, I'm so glad you forgot to put the firing caps in. Could you deliver this stuffed gerbil to the Prince, and bid him please accept it from Aglaya with her most unwavering respect. I'll pay you later.

IPPOLIT. *(with a cough)* Within the year, I hope.

AGLAYA. Go, go!

MME. YEPANCHIN. *(grabbing the stuffed gerbil from* **IPPOLIT***)* Aglaya! What is the meaning of this stuffed gerbil?

AGLAYA. It's a stuffed gerbil I'm sending the Prince. *(exits)*

MME. YEPANCHIN. It symbolizes something, child – you've been reading literature again!

*(Tremolo music: **STUFFÉD GERBIL**.*

She holds the stuffed gerbil aloft to **IPPOLIT** *:)*

There seems to be a motif of gerbils in the air ….

(sings:)

WHAT MEANS THIS STUF-FED GERBIL?

AGLAYA. *(entering, singing:)*

PUTTING THE PAW ON MAN'S ANIMAL NATURE?

GANYA, IVOGLIN, LEBEDEV & IPPOLIT. *(as the former three enter; singing:)*

IS THE SOUL NO MORE THAN THIS OVER-PUFFED FURBALL?

ALL.

IS THAT WHAT WE'RE TRYING TO SAY HERE?

GERBIL,
GERBIL GERBIL GERBIL:
SYMBOL OF LIFE'S GNAWING MYSTERY!
POOR DUMB THING,
JUST ONE SQUEAL FROM YOU'D REVEAL
ALL THE RUMBLING
MESSAGE OF DOSTOYEVSKY!

AGLAYA.

BUT NO!
NOT A BURBLE!

MME. YEPANCHIN.

DEAD SILENT AND SERENE.

IVOGLIN & LEBEDEV.

CARCASS OF DARKNESS AND NONSENSE!

MME. YEPANCHIN & AGLAYA.

KEEPER OF DEEPER SIGNIFICANCE!

ALL.

GERBIL!

STUF-FED GERBIL! ...

WHAT COULD YOU POSSIBLE MEAN??

(MME. YEPANCHIN shoos everyone out except AGLAYA. MYSHKIN enters.)

MME. YEPANCHIN. Prince Myshkin – I demand to know the meaning of this stuffed gerbil from Aglaya!

MYSHKIN. It's a stuffed gerbil Aglaya's sending me to show that she thinks enough of me to send me a stuffed gerbil.

AGLAYA. And I suppose you know what this all means, Prince...we must marry as soon as possible.

MME. YEPANCHIN. Good God, the world is ending!

MYSHKIN. Could I marry you?

MME. YEPANCHIN. I refuse! I refuse!

AGLAYA. *(screaming)* Maman!! Behave yourself!!

(MME. YEPANCHIN cowers.)

Now, Prince. *(sweetly)* As the legal representative of my mother's only marriageable daughter, I must ask you some practical questions. How do you intend to support me?

MYSHKIN. I have every intention of making you happy forever. I will perhaps work as a tutor.

AGLAYA. Excellent – and during the summer you could get a part-time job as a professional athlete.

MYSHKIN. A profess –

AGLAYA. *(bursting out in semi-hysterical laughter)* Oh God – I'm sorry – I can't help myself.

MME. YEPANCHIN. *(relieved)* I thought so – another joke – I knew it from the start – from the gerbil. Apologize, child.

AGLAYA. I can't – I'll die laughing...I'm a brat. You're lovely and I do enjoy you so. Forgive me – *(sincerely)* I'm so young.

MME. YEPANCHIN. Prince Myshkin –

AGLAYA. Don't mention that name! He smells! He drools! He looks at me! *(runs off)*

MME. YEPANCHIN. *(sighing, looking fondly at* **MYSHKIN***)* I suppose I shall have to show you her dowry now. It's obvious she thinks of you in various romantic ways. *(displays a vase to* **MYSHKIN***)* This is our most precious heirloom. Long ago, the head of the Myshkin line dictated in his will that the last of the Prince Myshkins have his brain placed in this vase. An old family joke. Someday, I'm sure, I know some day you and Aglaya will pass it on to your son and laugh about it as much as you and I have just now at this moment. *(She is not laughing.)* Excuse me – I must go tell the cook about the wedding.

(She exits; **MYSHKIN**, *looking at the vase.* **AGLAYA** *sneaks up behind him.)*

AGLAYA. Don't break that vase!

*(***MYSHKIN*** starts, almost drops the vase;* **AGLAYA** *laughs.)*

MYSHKIN. Aglaya, everything you say is prophecy!

AGLAYA. I'll never marry you. You're as much a stranger to me as to everyone else.

(Suddenly kisses **MYSHKIN** *passionately, then kisses the vase.)*

I'll marry you, Prince Lyov. But not until I confront Natasha Fillipovna and get her out of your mind once and for all.

*(MUSIC: **THE OPERA**.*

ROGOZHIN *escorts* **NATASHA** *in and remains.*

NATASHA *and* **AGLAYA** *confront each other.*

The following is sung:)

AGLAYA.

NATASHA FILLIPOVNA!

NATASHA.

AGLAYA YAY-PUMPKIN!

NATASHA & AGLAYA.

I DESPISE YOU!!!

AGLAYA.

THE GNATS FROM YOUR WOMB
GAD ABOUT YOUR PERFUME
AND GO MAD AND MATE ON THE FLY–
THEY HISS THEN THEY POP THEN THEY DIE –
AND IN THEIR STRANGE INSECTUAL FASHION,
THEY'VE COVERED THE RANGE OF YOUR PASSION!

NATASHA.

THAT'S A GOOD LITTLE GIRL,
GOOD AS A WELL-KEPT ABBEY:
FECKLESSLY NEAT WHILE ROACHES EAT
FILET OF BABY
IN ALL THE REAL PLACES OF THE WORLD!

WHAT DO YOU NEED A MAN FOR –
MARRIAGE!
HA HAHAHA HA HAHAHA!
ALL YOU NEED IS A JANITOR
TO AIR OUT YOUR CAGE!

I TAKE BACK EVERYTHING I SAID IN THAT LETTER!

MYSHKIN.

AGLAYA, PLEASE! YOU'VE UPSET HER!

AGLAYA.

IF I HAD MY CHANCE I'D BEHEAD HER!

(struggles with **NATASHA***)*

ROGOZHIN. *(to* **AGLAYA***)*

BABY, I DON'T THINK YOU'D BETTER!

NATASHA.

HA HAHA HAHA HAHA HAHA!
YOU'RE AS WEAK AS A TITTER
WITHOUT YOUR MAID, MY DEAR –

AGLAYA.

HAHAHA HAHAHA HAHAHA HAHAHA!

NATASHA.

BUT I'VE ONLY TO ORDER
AND I'M OBEYED –
LOOK HERE!
ROGOZHIN!
GO!!

(**ROGOZHIN** *starts to go.*)

AGLAYA.

NO NO!
NO NO!!

ROGOZHIN. *(facing* **MYSHKIN***)*

MYSHKIN …

(with resignation, indicating **NATASHA***)*

SHE ENJOYS PLAYING CARDS IN THE KITCHEN,
AND PREFERS THE DOG-STYLE POSITION.

(exits)

MYSHKIN.

NATASHA! AGLAYA!

NATASHA & **AGLAYA.**

PICK, PRINCE,
BETWEEN US!
QUICK, PRINCE,
YOU PROMISED!
WHO SHALL REIGN
OVER ALL
YOUR BRAIN?

AGLAYA.

WHO WILL DO MORE GOOD FOR YOU?

NATASHA.

WHO CAN YOU DO MORE GOOD FOR?

NATASHA & **AGLAYA.**

TELL HER, PRINCE –
I'M THE ONLY ONE IN THE WORLD!

NATASHA. *(to* **MYSHKIN***)*
>   SHE'S WEAK –
>   YOU MUST
>   LEAVE HER –

*(***NATASHA*** faints in* **MYSHKIN***'s arms;* **AGLAYA** *squeals.)*

AGLAYA. *(overcome by the whole scene)*
>   I THINK
>   I'M GETTING
>   ...A FEVER.

(She begins a faint exit.)

MYSHKIN. *(dazed, cradling* **NATASHA***'s head and hair, carefully:)*
>   ONE
>   BIG
>   HAND
>   ON A THOUSAND HAIRS.
>   WHICH HAIR DO I FEEL?
>   THERE'S ONE,
>   THERE,
>   THERE.

(to the fading **AGLAYA***)*

UNDERSTAND!

(back to **NATASHA***)*

>   THERE,
>   THERE,
>   THERE.
>   I HARDLY
>   FEEL
>   A
>   HAIR ....

*(***AGLAYA** *is gone. Opera is over.*

NATASHA *awakens, shaking from a nightmare.)*

MYSHKIN. There, there. Be a child. We'll marry tomorrow.
I must see Aglaya and explain. I'll be back presently.

*(***NATASHA** *exits;* **MYSHKIN** *visits the* **YEPANCHINS***.)*

MME. YEPANCHIN. No! She's still delirious! You and I, Prince, we're very different. Excuse me, the cook is burning something. *(exits)*

(MUSIC: **COUNTERFEIT WEDDING MARCH.**

MYSHKIN *distraughtly staggers down "the aisle" with* **NATASHA.** *The stoic congregation contains two veiled women and four top-hatted men.*

ROGOZHIN *is the priest. He lavaboes a milky fluid into the vase, which he will use as the consecration chalice for the ceremony.)*

LEBEDEV. *(with a noose)* Your best man, Prince! I couldn't find a ring, but I brought the rope. You're listening to me again, Prince, I can tell. I'll carry it around my neck. Here – if you want to say anything else to me, just pull. It's a good pet I am, Prince. Lead me around on the rope and I'm faithful forever.

ROGOZHIN. *(intoning for the congregation)*

OH ALL-KNOWING GOD, DIVINE EYE OF ALL IDEA –

CONGREGATION.

HAVE MEANING ON US.

ROGOZHIN. *(raising the chalice-vase)*

FOR THIS IS MY BRAINMILK –

(gives chalice to **NATASHA***)*

CONGREGATION.

TAKE YE AND DRINK!

ROGOZHIN. *(as* **NATASHA** *drinks)*

POUR OUT YOUR GODHEAD UNTO THIS MAN –

CONGREGATION.

THAT HE MAY BE KNOWN TO US.

ROGOZHIN.

THAT WE MAY APPROVE HIS MARRIAGE –

CONGREGATION. *(as* **MYSHKIN** *drinks)*

AND FIND HIM FIT!

ROGOZHIN.

IN THE NAME OF THE LOGIC,
AND OF THE BRAIN,
AND OF THE HOLY INSIGHT –

CONGREGATION.
  AH-MEN.
ROGOZHIN. *(spoken)* Rise, brother, and reveal thyself, we
  pray thee.

  (pause, as **CONGREGATION** *sits.)*

MYSHKIN. *(rising)* Many times enormous ideas possess me,
  wild clumps of words lying in my stomach like old
  dead operas. But I cannot bear to hear myself! I am
  only subject to fits, but you are subject to life. And so,
  my message, if spoken, would be as ineffectual as the
  greatest art of all time. My words at best are only worth
  repeating. Love life. Watch your minds. Think of all
  there is in a mere seed and then break open your
  hearts!

  *(flings the chalice-vase, shattering it; cello plays the
  sound of a fly; bass: thump, thump, thump…)*

AGLAYA. Who needs you? All you care about are the deep-
  est regions of people's souls. Do you think we enjoy
  you rummaging around in our fondest, most unforgiv-
  able secrets? You're a cold prophet, Prince. One warm
  day you'll freeze to death!

MME. YEPANCHIN. Nothing but a vase. Nothing but some
  priceless heirloom some person or another knocked
  over. This is only a glass joke. But people, people fall
  apart every day. Why, this very moment bodies are
  decomposing madly all over the world.

MYSHKIN. You forgive me? Not only for the vase, but
  for everything? I love your face – it's absurd!
  Ridiculousness!

  (MUSIC: reprise of **FITTING**.*)*

  The root of all forgiveness, the truest light of love!
  The very foundation of life in the world. Sanity itself
  is merely the byproduct of a ridiculously insane com-
  plex of brain processes. Why, just think of the zillions
  of excited synaptic transactions it must take to create,
  say, catatonia!! Ridiculous! I embrace your glorious sil-
  liness! It is absurdity that makes us infinite! It is God
  that gives life meaninglessness!! For it is exactly what we

don't know that gives us perfect reason to go on living. what a burden it would be to know everything! Our brains would have no reason to move! Time crashes, space cracks, and light turns into marble. I eat! I eat! I eat our infinite absurdities! *(going to* **NATASHA***)* Thank brainless God we have no reason... *(pause: the aura.)* to be...what we are... *(As he takes* **NATASHA** *in his arms, he begins shaking, fitting.)*

NATASHA. *(screaming)* ROGOZHIN!!

*(***ROGOZHIN*** yanks* **NATASHA** *our of* **MYSHKIN***'s hold.* **MYSHKIN** *has a grand mal seizure.* **ROGOZHIN** *jumps on him to restrain him.* **LEBEDEV** *beats the rope on the floor.* **MYSHKIN** *almost strangles* **ROGOZHIN***.* **NATASHA** *screams again.)*

ROGOZHIN!!

*(***MYSHKIN*** releases* **ROGOZHIN***, and continues his fit.* **ROGOZHIN** *takes* **NATASHA** *to his house and lays her out dead. All but* **LEBEDEV** *have exited as* **MYSHKIN** *finishes.)*

(Music climaxes, sound of a fly, the fit dies. **LEBEDEV** *dangles the rope of his noose toward* **MYSHKIN***.)*

LEBEDEV. Just pull my rope, master! I'll make you a man out of monkey sperm!

MYSHKIN. *(counting clouds)* One...

LEBEDEV. I'll make a rope out of his spinal cord and give it to a child.

MYSHKIN. Two!

LEBEDEV. *(offering* **MYSHKIN** *the rope)* Here, baby, baby! It's just a long nipple on my neck. Count to three and suck out my head.

MYSHKIN. Three!

LEBEDEV. Goodbye, sweet little donkey. *(He barks and runs off.)*

MYSHKIN. I count four clouds today. Anthills! ...Natasha? One hundred twelve ants. *(examines his brain)* Twelve, thirteen thoughts in a row...and there's some more! *(looks up)* Sixteen clouds now.

(He begins counting everything at once, until **ROGOZHIN** *comes up to him.)*

ROGOZHIN. Brother. Come.

MYSHKIN. Rogozhin... *(pointing up)* The clouds aren't making a single picture...Is Natasha at your house?

ROGOZHIN. *(leading* **MYSHKIN***)* Yes. Here we are. Quiet as stones now.

MYSHKIN. Paryfon –

ROGOZHIN. *(having a chat)* I noticed you outside – so I addressed you and brought you here, and that's all I've been doing recently up to now.

MYSHKIN. That's true...Natasha...?

ROGOZHIN. She's in there...I slit her throat. On the bed. Behind the curtain.

MYSHKIN. *(having gotten up to look)* I can barely see...oh yes ...I found it...

ROGOZHIN. Prince, you'd better not have a fit. We can't afford screaming.

MYSHKIN. You've covered everything but her foot. Why her foot?

ROGOZHIN. Because if people hear you, and come in here, and see the body in that condition, I'd be arrested within a week.

MYSHKIN. *(crouching)* Paryfon – I'm fairly certain I can get up...I have in times past gotten up, often from a similar position...it's the fear. We must wait. It'll pass. ... When will she start smelling?

ROGOZHIN. I thought of that! I thought of covering her with flowers, but...that would be sad to see her covered with flowers...you know?

MYSHKIN. The knife, right? Your "letter opener?"

(They exchange laughs.)

ROGOZHIN. Below her breast – near the heart, you know? It went in, right? Three inches...maybe five inches ... you know?

MYSHKIN. *(hearing someone?)* Shh! People! ...Four people. *(pause)* I thought you cut her throat.

ROGOZHIN. She took poison.

MYSHKIN. She should start smelling any second now. It's very close in here.

ROGOZHIN. *(sniffing)* Yes – there it is now. *(gives* **MYSHKIN** *a deck of cards)* These are the cards we always used.

MYSHKIN. I wanted to see them. *(looks at them)* Again and again – I'm not saying what I should be saying. I did so want to see these, but – Rogozhin? Rogozhin – look! *(the cards fly, shower from his hand)* No use at all!! Like the one moment before the fit stretched out forever like the sun over the sky I remember my life –

(his eyes go distant; the cello plays a fly, starting and lighting fitfully; the bass thumps erratically)

ROGOZHIN. *(cradled by* **MYSHKIN**, *who from time to time caresses him blankly)* Did you know she was blind in one eye?! When she was sixteen, she saw two wolves eat a horse. She still has the bones! *(laughs)* … Smell that? I can hear her decomposing! *(listens closely)* Dp! Dp! Dp! Foom! Hear that, worms? *(pulls out his knife against a worm attack)* Try and get her worms … if you dare!! I should get five years…mentally unfit, you know? …You see…you hear…you smell…. "Stab!" she'd say, and I'd stab. "Bark! Bark!" she'd say and I'd…

*(***ROGOZHIN*** kisses ***NATASHA***'s dead mouth and howls insanely. The rest of the characters – save* **MME. YEPANCHIN** *- enter, barking at* **MYSHKIN**. *Soon* **ROGOZHIN** *begins barking, too.*

The MUSIC grows stealthily.

NATASHA *is revived by* **ROGOZHIN**'s *barking, and she begins yipping.* **NATASHA** *and* **ROGOZHIN** *turn their barking on* **MYSHKIN**. **NATASHA** *pulls off* **MYSHKIN**'s *left shoe and sock and begins gnawing his foot.* **MYSHKIN** *blank,* **ROGOZHIN** *still growling.*

The other characters put a glass cube over **MYSHKIN**. *His shoe and sock remain outside.* **MYSHKIN** *is now sitting cross-legged in the same place he began the play.)*

ROGOZHIN. *(his roaring turning into his final sentence)* Ro – ro – Rogozhin gets five years.

(He freezes, staring idiotically, deadly, at **MYSHKIN**, *as everyone ends up doing after his or her next line.)*

IPPOLIT. Ippolit dies of turberculosissss.

IVOGLIN. General Ivoglin dies of a stoke-kk-kk-kk!

GANYA. Ganya goes on as usual. As usual.

NATASHA. Natasha remains dead.

LEBEDEV. Lebedev hangs himself.

AGLAYA. Aglaya survives, and runs off with a lofty spasmodic heterosexual of almost saintly chastity.

MME. YEPANCHIN. Madame Yepanchin, the one good character in the story, sends the Prince to a Swiss mental clinic, where he never recovers, barely moves ... except for one day when he points to his eye and says –

MYSHKIN. Aaaaa –

MME. YEPANCHIN. But he was probably just trying to rub it, probably saying no more than –

MYSHKIN. Aaaaa –

MME. YEPANCHIN. And she finally breaks down, visits the Prince in Switzerland, and speaks the final lines of the show. *(to the ogling statues around the glass cage:)* Well, come to your senses, you. He's not there. We're inside, encaged in glass around him. I'm going home. Enough of these illusions!

(She starts to leave, freezes gracefully.

Everyone catatonic, reflecting on **MYSHKIN**.

The music dins them dims.

MYSHKIN *is heard droning "Aaaaa," or is it "I"?*

The music and the lights turn to nothing.)

OTHER TITLES AVAILABLE FROM SAMUEL FRENCH

MARIA/STUART

Jason Grote
Inspired by Freidrich Schiller's *Mary Stuart*

Dramatic Comedy / 1m, 5f / Multiple Sets

Up-and-coming cartoonist Stuart fights to keep the lid on his mother's and aunts' simmering angst. But the family's secrets channel themselves into a bizarre shapeshifter that guzzles soda, communicates by fax, and spouts old German verse. Friedrich Schiller's classic tale of warring queens inspires this gothic romp through the weirder side of suburban America.

"Grote has made a name for himself in recent years with scripts that explode the boundaries between the ordinary and the chimerical, the political and the aesthetic, the intimate and the dizzyingly cosmic."
– The Washington Post

"An ingenious tale, and mined with offbeat, explosive devices."
– The Seattle Times

"Absolutely astonishing. Tremendous writing, incredible acting. And laughs. Big laughs."
– DC Theatre Scene

"Crazily entertaining comedy…surreal, witty, expertly performed. *Maria/Stuart* is a mélange of intense, ludicrous, silly, common-garden-variety family hell. It is more than enough for a great night out at the theater."
– MetroWeekly

SAMUELFRENCH.COM

www.ingramcontent.com/pod-product-compliance
Lightning Source LLC
Chambersburg PA
CBHW070415120726
47909CB00005B/1666